DARK
HUNTER

THE HEADLESS
HUNTSMAN

First published 2015 by
A & C Black, an imprint of Bloomsbury Publishing Plc
50 Bedford Square, London, WC1B 3DP

www.bloomsbury.com

Bloomsbury is a registered trademark of Bloomsbury Publishing Plc

A CIP catalogue for this book is available from the British Library

ISBN 978–1-4729–0819-3

Printed and bound in Great Britain by CPI Group (UK) Ltd,
Croydon CR0 4YY

1 3 5 7 9 10 8 6 4 2

recommended by

www.catchup.org

Catch Up is a not-for-profit charity
which aims to address the problem of
underachievement that has its roots in
literacy and numeracy difficulties.

DARK HUNTER

THE HEADLESS HUNTSMAN

BENJAMIN HULME-CROSS

ILLUSTRATED BY NELSON EVERGREEN

A & C BLACK
AN IMPRINT OF BLOOMSBURY
LONDON NEW DELHI   NEW YORK   SYDNEY

The Dark Hunter

Mr Daniel Blood is the Dark Hunter.
People call him to fight evil demons,
vampires and ghosts.

Edgar and Mary help Mr Blood
with his work.

The three hunters need to be strong and
clever to survive...

Contents

Chapter 1

Goreditch

Mr Blood, Mary and Edgar walked along the main street of Goreditch. The streets were very dirty.

The people stood in small groups on the pavement. As Mr Blood passed them, some people turned their backs. Other people stared at him.

"I thought they would be happy to see us," Edgar said. "The letter said the town was under attack."

"And it said that we were their only hope," Mary added.

"We need to find the Sheriff," Mr Blood said.

They came to a large building with flags in front of it. "That must be the town hall," said Mary.

The town hall was guarded by several armed men.

"Stop!" one of the guards shouted as they came near. He and the other guards looked ready to fight. "What do you want?"

"I am the Dark Hunter," said Mr Blood. "The Sheriff asked us to come." The guards looked at each other and nodded.

"Follow me," said one of the guards. He unlocked the door and led them into the town hall. They walked across a hall and climbed some stairs to a door.

"This is the Sheriff's office," said the guard. He opened the door and let them in.

A group of well-dressed men stood by the fire. A short, round man with a fat belly came towards them.

"Are you the Dark Hunter?" he asked. Mr Blood nodded.

The Sheriff turned to the other men in the room. "We are saved!" he said.

"What is it that you need saving from?" asked Mr Blood. "Your letter said that you were in danger from a monster."

"He is a terrible monster," said the Sheriff. "He has killed many of us. He attacks at night. We call him the Headless Huntsman."

Chapter 2

The Graveyard

At the mention of a headless huntsman, Mary looked excited. Edgar looked scared.

"He has killed six people already," the Sheriff said. "He cuts off people's heads with an axe. And he means to kill us all, I know it!"

"You think he means to kill all the people of the town?" asked Mr Blood.

"No!" said the Sheriff. "He means to kill all the people of the town council. All the people in this room, Mr Blood. There are just six of us left."

"You have a monster who wants to kill the town council?" said Mr Blood. "Do you know why?"

"It doesn't matter why," the Sheriff replied. "The important thing is he must be stopped!"

"The Headless Huntsman comes every night before midnight," explained the Sheriff. "He comes from the graveyard on the moors. He wears hunting clothes and he carries an axe. Can you help us?"

"I will find him for you," said Mr Blood.

"You must destroy him!" the Sheriff cried.

* * *

Just before sunset, Mr Blood, Edgar and Mary left the town hall. The Sheriff had given them horses.

The people on the streets looked very angry.

"It seems to me," said Mr Blood, "that the people of Goreditch have no love for the town council!"

Edgar followed a map that the Sheriff had given them. They rode out of town and up a steep hill. Soon they were on the open moor.

They lit lanterns when it began to get dark. At last they reached the place that was marked "Graveyard" on the map. They left their horses by the roadside and walked around. It was a grim place but it didn't look much like a graveyard.

"Look," said Edgar, pointing at a hangman's noose hanging from a tree.

"But where are the gravestones?" Mary asked.

"There are none," said Mr Blood. "But this *is* a graveyard. Look!"

At his feet was a long pile of freshly dug earth.

"An unmarked grave," said Edgar.

Chapter 3

A Red Axe

Mary and Edgar followed Mr Blood as he walked around. There were lots of unmarked graves. But none of the others looked disturbed. They came back to the first grave they had seen.

"This must be where the Headless Huntsman is coming from," said Mary.

"So what are we going to do?" Edgar asked.

"We will wait," Mr Blood replied. "I can't kill a ghost. The only way to free the town from the ghost is to free the ghost. We must find out why he can't rest in peace."

"So we're going to talk to him!" Mary cried. She sounded excited.

"Do we have to?" asked Edgar.

They put their lanterns on the ground and sat around the tree waiting for the Headless Huntsman to appear. A strong wind was blowing across the moors and soon they were all feeling very cold.

"I'll get some wood for a fire," said Edgar. He went back to the road. He was stroking his horse's nose when something caught his eye.

He picked up his lantern to look more closely and then gave a cry of fear. Someone had painted a red axe on the horse's neck.

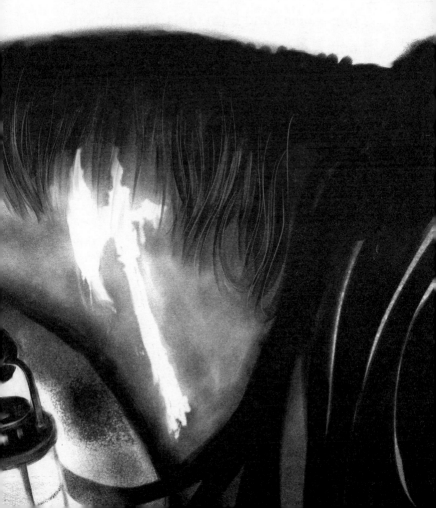

Edgar turned to go back but, as he did so, he saw a mob of men marching up the road towards him. Some of them carried torches. The rest had weapons – clubs, spears and farm tools. One of them pointed at Edgar. The mob began running towards him, shouting.

Edgar rushed back to Mary and
Mr Blood. In the moonlight he could just
see Mary hiding behind the tree. Mr Blood
stood at one end of the grave. At the other
end of the grave stood a big man holding
an axe. The man had no head!

"Mr Blood!" shouted Edgar, "Men with weapons. I think they're coming for us!"

Mr Blood swore. The moon went behind a cloud. When it shone through again, a second later, the Huntsman had vanished.

"Run!" Mr Blood shouted. The three of them raced back to the horses. Edgar's horse had gone. He scrambled up on Mary's horse, sitting behind her. The mob yelled as Mary and Mr Blood rode away as fast as they could.

Behind them they heard a cheer and then the mob began to chant:

"*Hail to the Huntsman! Hail to the Huntsman!*"

Chapter 4

The Huntsman

"That mob must have come from the town," said Edgar as they rode. "And they don't want us to get rid of the Huntsman."

"It sounds almost like they worship him," said Mary.

"They are grateful to me," someone said behind them.

Mr Blood and Mary turned their horses around.

The Headless Huntsman sat on Edgar's horse in the middle of the road. Edgar was so afraid, he could hardly breathe. He could feel Mary trembling.

"Why do you kill?" Mr Blood
demanded. "How did you die?"

The Huntsman made a chopping
movement with his hand through the air
where his head should have been.

"You were executed," said Mr Blood.

"And you seek revenge."

"No," the Huntsman replied. "I seek justice. The men of the council take everything for themselves, while the people are starving. I told them this was wrong, and they had me killed. The town does not need to be freed from me but from the council."

The Huntsman began to ride up a small hill. "Follow me," he called. They all rode in silence to the top of the hill. The clouds had gone and the moon shone bright over Goreditch.

"You can see thirteen large buildings in the town," the Huntsman went on. "One is the town hall. The others were built as homes by each of the twelve councillors. They tax the people and keep the money. They pay their guards well enough so nobody dares to take them on. Until now."

"Let us come with you," said Mr Blood. "Before you kill them, let me try to reason with them."

"It is too late for that," said the Huntsman. He kicked the horse's sides and galloped off down the hill towards Goreditch.

Chapter 5

Justice

Mr Blood, Edgar and Mary followed the Huntsman. They were not on the road and the mob did not see them. As they got near to the town they could hear shouts and screams coming from the town hall.

A crowd of people stood outside. "Hail to the Huntsman! Hail to the Huntsman!" they chanted. Three guards lay dead on the ground. Their heads were missing.

"People of Goreditch!" Mr Blood called. "I know that the Council has brought evil on this town. But. . ."

The crowd turned to Mr Blood. There was rage on every face.

"They'll kill us!" shouted Edgar. He, Mary and Mr Blood jumped off their horses and ran to the town hall doors.

"Let them go in!" someone shouted. "The Huntsman will deal with them!"

They bolted the doors behind them and raced up to the Sheriff's office. Inside they found the Sheriff and four of the councillors standing by the opposite wall. Their faces were grey with fear.

"Mr Blood!" the Sheriff cried. "Thank Heavens! The Huntsman dragged each of us from our beds and brought us here. Save us!"

At that moment the door opened and the Huntsman came in. He dumped another of the councillors on the floor and the man crawled over to his friends.

"Killers and thieves!" the Huntsman roared. "This ends tonight!"

"Wait!" cried Mr Blood. "If you want the people of Goreditch to be free, then they must free themselves. Hand the councillors over to the people. Let the people decide what to do with them."

Very well," said the Huntsman. "Come with me." He led Mr Blood and the children back out onto the street. A roar went up from the crowd. The Huntsman waited for it to die down, then spoke.

"Friends," the Huntsman said to the crowd. His voice seemed to be coming from everywhere. "I know the councillors have destroyed many lives in this town. That is why I have taken their lives in return."

The crowd cheered and shouted, "*Hail to the Huntsman! Hail to the Huntsman!*"

"Now it is for you to decide what happens to the councillors. Should I kill them all?" asked the Headless Huntsman.

Then, Mary spoke up. "Make them pay for their evil deeds but let them live. If you spill more blood it will bring shame on you all."

"Well said, Mary," whispered Mr Blood.

Then, the crowd all began to talk at once. A young man ran to the top of the Town Hall steps.

"The girl is right," he shouted to the crowd.

"We are better than the councillors. We will not make them pay with their lives but they will give their rich houses to the poor and they will work for the rest of their lives to make up for their greed and cruelty," he said.

"Yes! Yes!" shouted the crowd.

Mr Blood turned to the Headless Huntsman but he had vanished.

"What has happened to the Headless Huntsman?" asked Edgar, as the three of them left the town of Goreditch.

"Now he has brought justice to the town, he can rest in peace," said Mr Blood.